For Hope Alice White
— D.C.R.

To my parents
— M.M.

Text copyright © 1996 by Dian Curtis Regan
Illustrations copyright © 1996 by Mary Morgan
All rights reserved. Published by Scholastic Inc.
CARTWHEEL BOOKS and the CARTWHEEL BOOKS logo
are registered trademarks of Scholastic Inc.

Library of Congress Cataloging-in-Publication Data is available.

ISBN 0-590-47972-5

12 11 10 9 8 7 6 5 4 3 2 1   6 7 8 9/9 0 1/0

Printed in Singapore   46

First Scholastic printing, April 1996

M·O·M·M·I·E·S

by Dian Curtis Regan
Illustrated by Mary Morgan

SCHOLASTIC INC.
New York Toronto London Auckland Sydney

Wake up, Mommy, it's time to play.
Saturday's my favorite day.

First we rise
and exercise.

Find a cup, a bowl, a spoon.
Eat and watch a fun cartoon.

Mom can fasten. Mom can clip.
I can button. I can zip.

In the car, I sing a song.
Mommy likes to sing along.

At the park, a puppet show!
Dragons scare the crowd below.

In the pool,
we get cool.

Mom spreads a blanket; time to eat.
Apples make a crunchy treat.

We drink lemonade,
and read in the shade.

Swing low; swing high.
Close my eyes and kiss the sky.

Hide and seek.
I don't peek.

Boo! It's me!
Behind a tree.

Sunset. Sky's aglow.
Time to pack our things and go.

Where's the car?
It isn't far.

Mommy helps shampoo and scrub.
We play puppets in the tub.

I whisper a riddle.

Mom tickles my middle.

Mommy makes noodles and bread.

Go upstairs; it's time for bed.

Jammies on; brush my hair.
A hug for me; a kiss for bear.

Click off the light.
Good night, good night.

Hug tight.